The Gift of Nothing

• PATRICK McDONNELL •

LITTLE, BROWN AND COMPANY
New York ᴕ Boston

Text and Illustration copyright © 2005 by Patrick McDonnell   Mutts © 2005 by Patrick McDonnell, distributed by King Features Syndicate   All rights reserved.

Little, Brown and Company • Time Warner Book Group • 1271 Avenue of the Americas, New York, NY 10020 • Visit our Web site at www.lb-kids.com

Library of Congress Cataloging-in-Publication Data: McDonnell, Patrick. The gift of nothing / by Patrick McDonnell.— 1st ed.   p. cm.

Based on the author's comic strip, Mutts. Summary: Mooch the cat tries to think of a gift to give his friend Earl the dog.   ISBN 0-316-11488-X

[1. Gifts—Fiction. 2. Friendship—Fiction. 3. Cats—Fiction. 4. Dogs—Fiction.] I. McDonnell, Patrick. Mutts. II. Title.

PZ7.M1554Gi 2005   [E]—dc22   2005002584

First Edition: October 2005   10 9 8 7 6 5 4 3 2 1   PHX   Printed in the U.S.A.   Printed on recycled paper

It was a special day

and Mooch

wanted to give his best friend, Earl, a gift.

But what to get him?

He had a bowl.

He had a bed.

He had a chewy toy.

He had it ALL.

Mooch thought and thought.

What do you get someone who has everything?

NOTHING!

He would give Earl the gift of nothing.

But in this world filled with so many somethings, where could he find nothing?

Mooch often heard Frank say there was "nothing on TV."

But as far as Mooch could tell,
there was always something on TV.

Mooch often heard Doozy and her friends say
there was "nothing to do."

But as far as Mooch could tell,
everybody was always doing something.

Millie came home from the store and said,
"There was nothing to buy!"

So Mooch went shopping.

Mooch looked up and down every aisle.
He found many, many, many somethings.

The latest this, the newest that . . .

but as far as he could tell, nothing was not for sale.

So Mooch went home

and sat on his pillow

and just stayed still (as cats often do).

And not looking for it, he found

PURRRL...

nothing.

So he went and got a box

and put nothing in it.

Then Mooch thought, *Hmmm* . . .
maybe Earl deserves more than this.

So he got a bigger box.

"Now that's plenty of nothing!"

"For me?" said Earl.
"Mooch, you didn't have to give me anything."

Who told him? thought Mooch.

Earl opened Mooch's gift.

"There's nothing here," said Earl.

"Yesh!" said Mooch. "Nothing...

"but me and you."

So Mooch and Earl just stayed still

and enjoyed nothing